The Dog and the Dolphin

By

James B. Dworkin

Illustrated by

Michael Chelich

ISBN: 1494702541
ISBN-13: 9781494702540
Library of Congress Control Number: 2013923455
CreateSpace Independent Publishing Platform
North Charleston, South Carolina

www.thedogandthedolphin.com

Red, an Irish Setter, is spending a lazy day on a beautiful beach.

He sniffs the shells
on the beach,

and looks out at the waves
on the water.

Red chases
the seagulls and
the pelicans.

He watches the parasailors,

hot air balloons, sailboats,

and the airplanes

and helicopters.

But Red is very sad, as he has no friends to play with.

Then, he looks out at the water again.

What is it that he sees?

A shark or swordfish?

NO!!

A sea monster?

NO!!!

Red runs out to
the water's edge for
a closer look.

Why, it is a
very playful
dolphin!

Red is so happy to
finally have a friend to
play with at the beach.

Red runs down the beach

as the dolphin swims along!

"Oops!"

"Where did you go?"

"Here you are!"

"Whee!"

The dolphin plays keep away from the dog with a Frisbee.

Oh, it is getting late.
The sun is going down.

The dolphin
waves good-bye
with his fin.

Red dries off and barks
a loud good-bye to his
newfound friend.

Red and the dolphin are
tired from their long day
of playing.

They both hope to see each other again tomorrow because they have become best friends.

The end.

James B. Dworkin is an educator who is based in Indiana. The author is currently the chancellor at Purdue University North Central, a position he has held for fourteen years. His work has been recognized with several awards, and he was recently honored by being named a Sagamore of the Wabash by Governor Mike Pence of Indiana. Dworkin is the author of two books, and has published more than eighty articles on labor economics and labor relations. *The Dog and the Dolphin* is his first children's book. Visit www.thedogandthedolphin.com to learn more about this story.

Michael Chelich is a fine artist/illustrator living in Northwest Indiana. Michael paints a variety of subject matter including portraiture, still life, narrative figurative painting, landscape, wildlife and pet portraits. He has been published in several national art magazines including American Artist, The Artist's Magazine, and the Classical Realism Journal. See more of his artwork at Michaelchelich.com